Little Lamb
to the Rescue

Written by Erica Briers ✻ Illustrated by Stephanie Boey

TEMPLAR

It was spring and out in the green fields

Little Lamb was struggling to her feet. This was her first day in the world and she was very excited to be alive.

She stood up on her wobbly legs and looked around her.

Lots of other lambs had been born in the same field as Little Lamb, but each one was different—some were black all over, some were white all over, and some were a mixture. Little Lamb was mostly white, but she had lovely black ears, a black nose, and black feet so it looked like she was wearing socks!

All the other lambs were different sizes too, but Little Lamb was the littlest of them all. But, although she was small, she had a big heart, and wanted more than anything to be useful. She decided to set off around the farm to see what she could do.

That day, the sheep were being rounded up ready to have their woolly coats sheared.

"Please can I come too?" asked Little Lamb.

"Not yet," said her father, the big curly-horned ram. "You are still far too small to be sheared, you don't have enough wool. Run along and play, Little Lamb."

So Little Lamb went to see the chickens. The farm dog was there, watching over the newly-hatched chicks, just in case the fox came prowling around..

"Please can I help?" asked Little Lamb.

But the farm dog just said kindly, "You are so tiny that I think the fox might eat you as well as the chicks!"

"Little Lamb, Little Lamb!" cried the farm ducklings as she walked past the pond. "You're far too small to help anyone at all!"

And the cheeky little ducklings waddled along after her, laughing and quacking until poor Little Lamb ran away into the meadow.

Poor **Little Lamb**! She sat down in the daisy patch, feeling miserable and unwanted.

Then, among the buzzing of the bees and the rustle of the grass, she heard a faint **cheeping** noise. Little Lamb followed the sound to the base of a shady tree. There, amongst the long grass and stinging nettles, was a fluffy **baby bird**.

"Please can you help me?" cheeped the baby bird, miserably. "I have fallen from my nest in the tree, and I am worried that the fox might find me soon!"

"I'm afraid not," said Little Lamb, "For I'm too small to help anyone at all!"

But the baby bird cheeped so sadly that Little Lamb knew she had to do something.

So Little Lamb leant right **down** to the ground.
And the baby bird hopped right up onto her head.
Then Little Lamb carefully put her front feet on the
fence and stretched **higher** and **higher** until...

...the baby bird hopped right back into his nest.

The baby bird was very happy to be back with his brothers and sisters. And the baby bird's mother was very pleased to have him safely back home.

"Thank you Little Lamb," she said. "You are the kindest, most helpful animal on this farm. We hope you will always be around to help us!"

And all the baby birds chirped noisily in agreement!

Little Lamb was so happy to have found someone to help! She ran off to tell the other lambs all about it, hopping and skipping through the daisies, and shaking her tail in delight as she went.

So Little Lamb went to see the big farm horse, who was about to take the farmer to market in the farm cart.

"Please can I help?" asked Little Lamb.

"Oh no," snorted the horse. "You are *far* too *little* to pull this great, big cart…"

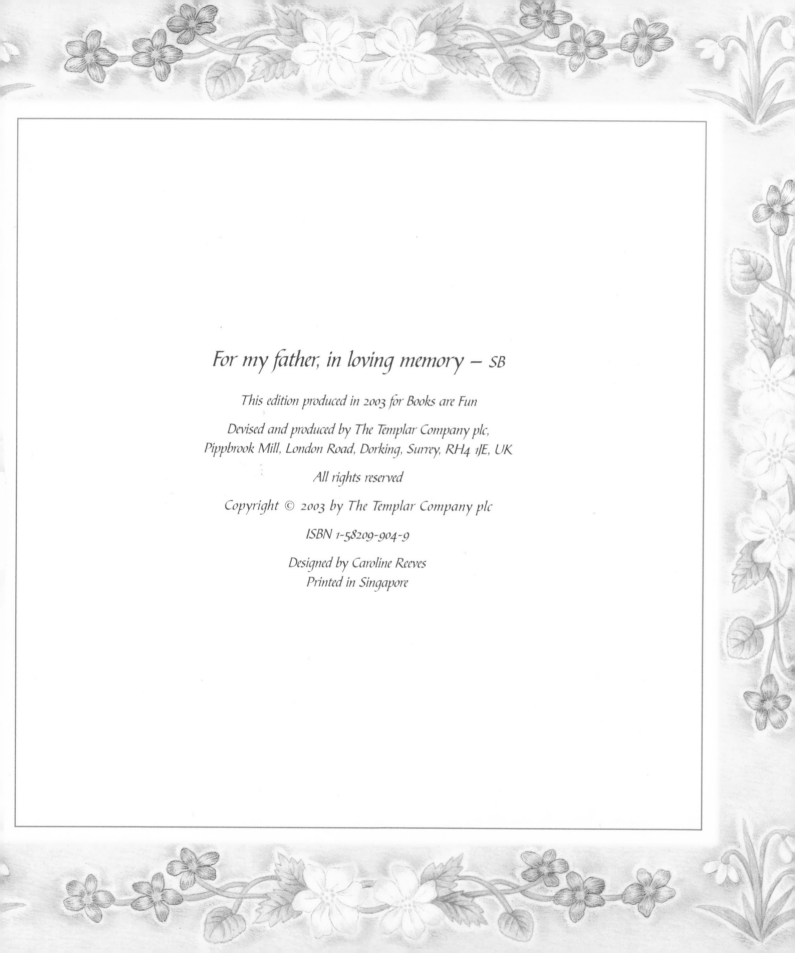

For my father, in loving memory – SB

This edition produced in 2003 for Books are Fun

Devised and produced by The Templar Company plc,
Pippbrook Mill, London Road, Dorking, Surrey, RH4 1JE, UK

ISBN 1-58209-904-9

Designed by Caroline Reeves
Printed in Singapore